MR. BUSY

by Roger Hargreaves

WORLD INTERNATIONAL

There has never been anybody quite like Mr Busy.

He could do things ten times as fast as ever you or I could.

For instance, if he was reading this book, he'd have finished it by now.

He lived in a very busy-looking house which he'd built himself.

As you can see.

It had lots of doors and windows, and do you know what it was called?

Weekend Cottage!

Do you know why?

Because that's how long it took him to build it!

One fine summer morning, Mr Busy was up and about bright and early at 6 o'clock.

He jumped out of bed and had a bath, and cleaned his teeth, and cooked his breakfast, and ate his breakfast, and read the paper, and washed up, and made his bed, and cleaned the house from top to bottom.

By which time it was 7 o'clock.

Busy Mr Busy!

Now, next door to Mr Busy lived someone who wasn't quite such a busy person.

In fact, a very unbusy person.

Mr Slow!

If he was reading this book he'd . . . read . . . it . . . like . . . this!

He'd still be on the first page!

And that same fine summer morning, at five past seven, when Mr Busy knocked at his door, Mr Slow was fast asleep in bed.

He'd gone to bed for an afternoon nap the day before, and somehow hadn't woken up until he heard Mr Busy knocking at his door.

"Who's . . . that . . . knocking . . . at . . . my . . . door?" he called downstairs.

"Good morning," cried Mr Busy. "Can I come in?"

And, without waiting for an answer, he went inside.

"Where are you?" he called.

"Up . . . stairs," came the slow reply.

So Mr Busy went upstairs, two at a time.

"Good heavens!" he said. "You're still in bed!"

And he made Mr Slow get up.

And he made his bed for him, and cooked his breakfast for him, and cleaned his house for him.

Poor Mr Slow.

He hated to be rushed and fussed.

"Right," said Mr Busy briskly. "It's a fine day. Let's go for a picnic."

Mr Slow pulled a face.

"I . . . don't . . . like . . . picnics," he complained.

"Nonsense," replied Mr Busy, and busied himself around Mr Slow's kitchen making up a picnic for the two of them.

It took him a minute and a half.

"Right," he cried when he'd finished. "Off we go!"

And he bustled Mr Slow out of his front door, and off they set.

As you can imagine, Mr Busy walks extremely quickly.

And, as you can imagine, Mr Slow doesn't.

So, by the time Mr Busy had walked a mile, do you know how far Mr Slow had walked?

To his own garden gate!

Mr Busy hurried back.

"Come on," he cried impatiently. "Hurry up!"

"Hurry . . . up?" replied Mr Slow.

"Im . . . poss . . . i . . . ble!"

"Oh, all right," said Mr Busy. "We'll have a picnic in your garden."

"Wait a minute, though," he added. "The grass needs cutting."

And he rushed back to Weekend Cottage and rushed back again with his lawnmower, and rushed up and down cutting Mr Slow's lawn.

It took him two and a half minutes!

It would have taken him two minutes, but he had to mow around Mr Slow who couldn't get out of the way in time.

"Right," cried Mr Busy. "Picnic time!"

And together on that fine summer day they had a fine picnic.

Well, actually, Mr Busy had a finer picnic than Mr Slow because he ate more quickly and had most of the food.

Mr Busy stretched out on the grass.

"That was fun," he said. "I like picnics!"

"You . . . do! . . . I . . . don't," said Mr Slow.

"Tell you what," went on Mr Busy, ignoring him. "Tomorrow we'll go on a proper picnic, out in the country."

Mr Slow pulled a face.

"And," went on Mr Busy, "in order to do that and get you out into the country, I'll have to call for you earlier than I did this morning."

Mr Slow pulled another face.

"See you tomorrow then," said Mr Busy, and went home and cleaned his house from bottom to top.

The following morning, Mr Busy jumped out of bed at 5 o'clock and had a bath and cleaned his teeth, and cooked his breakfast, and ate his breakfast, and read the paper, and washed up, and made his bed, and cleaned the house from top to bottom.

By which time it was 6 o'clock.

He went and knocked on Mr Slow's front door.

"Come on! Come on!" he cried. "Time to be up and about! Picnic day!"

No reply.

"Come on!" cried Mr Busy again.

No reply.

Mr Busy went inside.

And went upstairs, three at a time, and into Mr Slow's bedroom, expecting to find him in bed.

But he wasn't.

And he wasn't anywhere upstairs.

And he wasn't anywhere downstairs.

"Bother," said Mr Busy. "I wonder where he's got to?"

Where Mr Slow had got to was under his bed.

Hiding!

He didn't want to go on any picnic.

Not he.

"Bother," said Mr Busy again. "That means I'll have to go on a picnic on my own!"

Under his bed, Mr Slow smiled a slow smile.

"What . . . a . . . good . . . idea," he said.

And went to sleep.

Snoring very slowly.

MORE SPECIAL OFFERS
FOR MR MEN AND LITTLE MISS READERS

In every Mr Men and Little Miss book like this one, <u>and now</u> in the Mr Men
sticker and activity books, you will find a special token. Collect six tokens and we
will send you a gift of your choice
Choose either a <u>Mr Men</u> or <u>Little Miss</u> poster, <u>or</u> a Mr Men or Little Miss
double sided full colour bedroom door hanger.

Return this page **with six tokens per gift required** to:
Marketing Dept., MM / LM, World International Ltd.,
PO Box 7, Manchester, M19 2HD

Your name:_____ Age: _____

Address: _____

_____

_____ Postcode: _____

Parent / Guardian Name (Please Print)_____

Please tape a 20p coin to your request to cover part post and package cost

I enclose <u>six</u> tokens per gift, and 20p please send me:-

<u>Posters:-</u>	Mr Men Poster ☐	Little Miss Poster ☐	
<u>Door Hangers</u> -	Mr Nosey / Muddle ☐	Mr Greedy / Lazy ☐	
	Mr Tickle / Grumpy ☐	Mr Slow / Busy ☐	
	Mr Messy / Quiet ☐	Mr Perfect / Forgetful ☐	
	L Miss Fun / Late ☐	L Miss Helpful / Tidy ☐	
	L Miss Busy / Brainy ☐	L Miss Star / Fun ☐	

20p

Stick 20p here please

We may occasionally wish to advise you of other Mr Men gifts. ☐
you would rather we didn't please tick this box

Please Tick Appropriate Box

├─ 100 mm ─┤

250 mm

ENTRANCE FEE
3 SAUSAGES

MR.GREEDY

Collect six of these tokens
You will find one inside every
Mr Men and Little Miss book
which has this special offer.

1
TOKEN

Offer open to residents of UK, Channel Isles and Ireland only

NEW

Full colour Mr Men and Little Miss Library Presentation Cases in durable, wipe clean plastic.

In response to the many thousands of requests for the above, we are delighted to advise that these are now available direct from ourselves,
for only **£4.99** (inc VAT) plus 50p p&p.
The full colour boxes accommodate each complete library. They have an integral carrying handle as well as a neat stay closed fastener.
Please do not send cash in the post. Cheques should be made payable to **World International Ltd. for the sum of £5.49** (inc p&p) per box.

Please note books are not included.

Please return this page with your cheque, stating below which presentation box you would like, to:
**Mr Men Office, World International
PO Box 7, Manchester, M19 2HD**

Your name:_____

Address: _____

_____

_____Postcode: _____

Name of Parent/Guardian (please print):_____

Signature:_____

I enclose a cheque for £_____ made payable to World International Ltd.,

Please send me a Mr Men Presentation Box ☐

           Little Miss Presentation Box ☐
     (please tick or write in quantity)
     and allow 28 days for delivery

Thank you

Offer applies to UK, Eire & Channel Isles only

Have you discovered the Little Miss books yet?
There are 30 to collect, and when you have
them all this is what you'll see!

Little Miss Giggles says,
"You'll laugh a lot with these little books!"

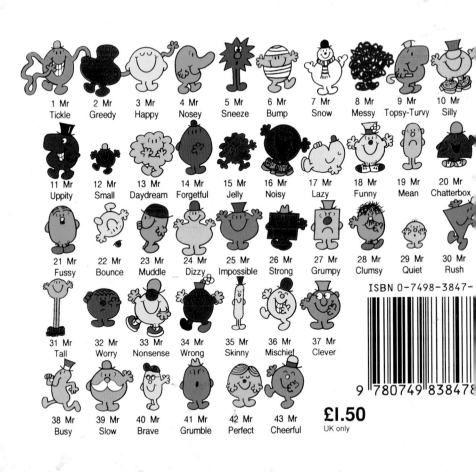

1 Mr Tickle
2 Mr Greedy
3 Mr Happy
4 Mr Nosey
5 Mr Sneeze
6 Mr Bump
7 Mr Snow
8 Mr Messy
9 Mr Topsy-Turvy
10 Mr Silly

11 Mr Uppity
12 Mr Small
13 Mr Daydream
14 Mr Forgetful
15 Mr Jelly
16 Mr Noisy
17 Mr Lazy
18 Mr Funny
19 Mr Mean
20 Mr Chatterbox

21 Mr Fussy
22 Mr Bounce
23 Mr Muddle
24 Mr Dizzy
25 Mr Impossible
26 Mr Strong
27 Mr Grumpy
28 Mr Clumsy
29 Mr Quiet
30 Mr Rush

31 Mr Tall
32 Mr Worry
33 Mr Nonsense
34 Mr Wrong
35 Mr Skinny
36 Mr Mischief
37 Mr Clever

38 Mr Busy
39 Mr Slow
40 Mr Brave
41 Mr Grumble
42 Mr Perfect
43 Mr Cheerful

ISBN 0-7498-3847-
9 780749 838478

£1.50
UK only